THE
STAR
IN THE
FOREST

HELEN KELLOCK

Thames & Hudson

Maisie and Pip sat in the snug warmth of their grandparents' cottage, deciding how to spend the first night of their vacation.

Pip was happy to wait and watch the stars appear one by one across the clear night sky.

But even though Maisie loved the stars as much as her big sister, she did NOT love waiting.

Maisie dreamed of something exciting.
A shiny new discovery! A SPECTACULAR adventure!

Stargazing and hot chocolate were not it.

As she stared out into space, she willed something to happen.

Suddenly, a bright flash
lit up the sky.
"What WAS that?"
Maisie squealed.

She sprang into action at once.
"Maybe it was a rocketship?
Or a creature from outer space?"

"Wait, Maisie!" shouted Pip.

"There's no time to wait!
We've got to find out!"

Maisie and Pip had often played in the forest,
but in the gloomy dusk everything looked different.

"Did you hear that?"
whispered Pip nervously.

"It's just a fox, Pip."

Maisie pressed ahead, as true adventurers do.
She chattered excitedly as they picked
their way through the tangle.

"What do you think it was that fell from the sky, Pip?
It lit up the forest like a sparkly jewel. It could be the biggest,
shiniest space jewel anyone has EVER seen!"

Pip stared up into the trees. She began to
wonder if she and Maisie were not alone...

"Look up, Maisie. Do you see something?" said Pip.

"It's just owls, Pip.
Come on, hurry up!"

They crawled through thickets.

They peered through hollows.

All they found were grubs and bugs...
But *something* had lit up the sky and Maisie
was determined to find out what.

From up high, Maisie spied a glow
in a clearing below.

"At last!"

Maisie jumped through the air
and ran like thunder.

"What could it be?"
she wondered wildly.

"Space jewels...
a UFO..."

But when at last Maisie reached the clearing
she found none of these.

"Pip?" she called out through the shadows.
"Pip...?"

Pip had followed behind at a
Pip-like pace, taking in the magic
of the forest around them.

"You found it! What is it?"

"It's just a lump of cold nothing," Maisie grumbled.
"Let's go home."

"Wait a minute,"
said Pip, peering closer.
"I think... I think it might
be a fallen star."

"A star?
Wow! A STAR!
You're right, Pip! It's a magical meteorite,
all the way from OUTER SPACE!"

Maisie followed Pip's wandering pace
back home. She looked up and finally saw
the glowing fireflies and heard the soft
hoot of the owls.

The forest, like their star, sparkled all around.

"I can't wait to find out what tomorrow's
adventure will be!" Maisie grinned.

For Wesley

The Star in the Forest © 2019 Thames & Hudson Ltd, London
Text and Illustrations © 2019 Helen Kellock

First published in the United States of America in 2019 by Thames & Hudson Inc.,
500 Fifth Avenue, New York, New York 10110

www.thamesandhudsonusa.com

Library of Congress Control Number 2019931891

ISBN 978-0-500-65190-2

Printed and bound in China by Leo Paper Products Ltd.

"A star?
Wow! A STAR!
You're right, Pip! It's a magical meteorite,
all the way from OUTER SPACE!"